DETROIT PUBLIC LIBRARY

DATE DUE

MAR 3 1 1994

SEP 0 2 1994

MAR 2 3 1995

OCT 2 6 1995

S0-BRC-584

FOX TALES

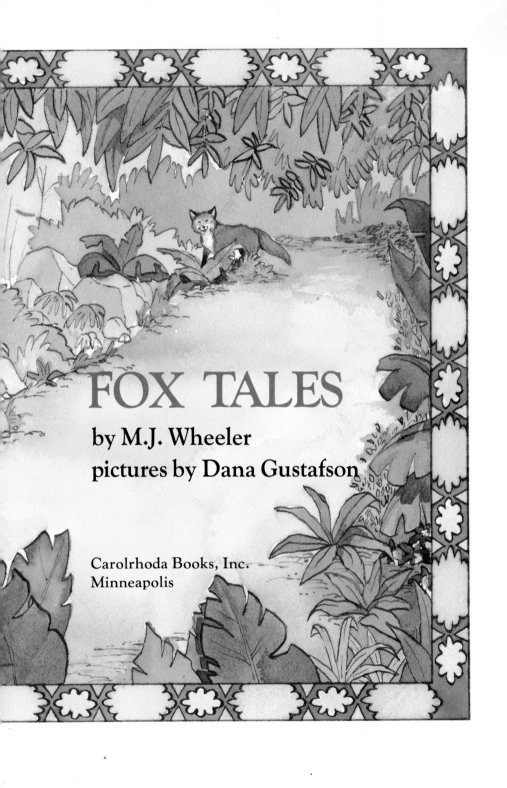

FOX TALES

by M.J. Wheeler
pictures by Dana Gustafson

Carolrhoda Books, Inc.
Minneapolis

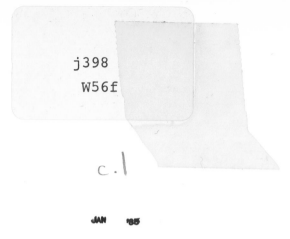

j398
W56f

c.1

JAN '85

Text copyright © 1984 by M.J. Wheeler
Pictures copyright © 1984 by Carolrhoda Books, Inc.
All rights reserved. International copyright secured. No part of this book may be
reproduced in any form whatsoever without permission in writing from the publisher
except for the inclusion of brief quotations in an acknowledged review.

Manufactured in the United States of America

Library of Congress Cataloging in Publication Data

Wheeler, M.J. (Mary Jo)
  Fox tales.

  Summary: A retelling of three Indian fables each fea-
turing the exploits of a fox. Included are "Whose Horse
Is It?," "The Bone Garden," and "The Stupid Fox."
  1. Fables, India. [1. Fables. 2. Folklore—India.
3. Foxes—Fiction] I. Gustafson, Dana, ill. II. Title.
PZ8.2.W49Fo 1984   398.2'452974442   83-21001
ISBN 0-87614-255-2 (lib. bdg.)

1 2 3 4 5 6 7 8 9 10 92 91 90 89 88 87 86 85 84

A Note from the Author

In India, outside the big cities, there is no television, little radio, few movies. For entertainment on long, hot afternoons and on quiet, moonlit nights, there are only the same old people—family and neighbors—whom one sees every day. But often one of these people is a storyteller. Then the magic of his words can make the everyday world grow dim and bring close distant times, high adventures, splendid kingdoms. Gods and goddesses speak, princes go to war, witches are punished. Sometimes, too, the stories are simpler ones like these—where tigers speak, humans try to trick each other, and foxes are almost always wise.

No one knows how old these stories are. They have been told for generations, passing from one storyteller to the next. In this retelling I have changed the Indian jackal to the more familiar fox, the oil seller (reputed in India to be especially untrustworthy) to a farmer, the credulous Brahmin to a simple man. But these changes, too, are in keeping with tradition. Every storyteller always uses his own words, adds his own ideas, and changes the story to please his own audience. As long as these stories are told and change, they remain both new and part of an ancient, continuing tradition.

For Mary Ann, Sarah, Isaac, and Ben

CONTENTS

Whose Horse
Is It?

Once a man was riding home on his horse.
He rode and he rode.
Night fell and still he was riding.
Then he saw a light
in the window of a farmhouse.
He got off his horse
and walked to the door.

"Ho there, is anyone home?" he called.
"Ho there to you, too,"
answered the farmer.
"What do you want?"
"I have come a long way.
I have been riding all day,"
said the traveler.
"May I sleep here tonight?"
"Come right in," said the farmer.
"You may sleep in here."
He showed the traveler to a bed.
"Please take good care of my horse,"
said the traveler.
"I still have a long way to go
before I get home."
"I'll take good care of him, all right,"
said the farmer.

The next morning
the traveler got ready to leave.
"Where is my horse?" he asked.
"Your horse ran away last night,"
said the farmer.
"It's too bad, but he is gone."
The traveler found this hard to believe.
He went outside to look around.
Sure enough, there was his horse,
near the barn.
"There is my horse," he said happily.
"No, that is my horse," said the farmer.
"Your horse!" said the traveler.
"Don't you think I know my own horse
when I see him? Besides, last night
you didn't have a horse at all."

"This is my horse," said the farmer.
"He wasn't here when you arrived
because he was born during the night."
"Where is his mother, then?"
asked the traveler.

"The barn is his mother,"
said the farmer.
"My barn had a baby horse last night,
and here he is."
He gave the horse a pat.

The traveler didn't believe this at all,
but what was he to do?
If he rode off on his horse,
the farmer would surely yell, "Thief!"
Then he had an idea.
"Is there a fox near here?" he asked.
"Of course there is,"
answered the farmer.
"We can go and ask the fox then,"
said the traveler.
"He will tell us whose horse this is."
"All right," said the farmer.
The farmer and the traveler
walked to the fox's den.
The fox was sitting at his front door,
smoking a pipe.
"Good day," he said.
"What can I do for you two?"

"Please tell me what to do,"
said the traveler.
"Last night I slept at this man's house.
He said he would take care of my horse,
but now he says my horse has run away.
I saw my horse next to his barn,
but he says it is his horse."

"Yes," said the farmer, "it *is* my horse.

It was born last night.

My barn is its mother."

"Go back to your farmhouse," said the fox.

"As soon as I have taken my bath,

I will come and see this horse.

Then I can tell you whose horse it is."

The farmer and the traveler
returned to the farmer's house.
They waited and waited,
but the fox did not come.
At last they went back to the fox's den.
There he was,
still sitting and smoking his pipe.
"Why didn't you come?" asked the farmer.
"We have been waiting for you
all day long."
"When I went to take my bath,
the water caught on fire from my pipe,"
said the fox.
"All day I have been working
to put out the fire."

"What do you mean?" shouted the farmer.
"Water cannot catch on fire.
I do not believe you."

"And I do not believe *you*," said the fox.
"A barn cannot be the mother of a horse."

Then the farmer knew
that he could not get away with his trick.
"All right," he said to the traveler,
"take your horse."
"Thank you, Fox," said the traveler.
And he got on his horse and rode away.

The Bone Garden

A peacock and a fox were friends.
Every day they ate together.
One day the peacock ate plums,
and the fox ate meat.
After he had finished his meal,
the peacock dug some holes
and buried the plum seeds.

"Why do you do that?" asked the fox.

"Don't you know anything?"

said the peacock.

"All the best animals do this.

These seeds will grow into plum trees.

Then I will always have

more plums to eat."

"Oh, of course," said the fox.

"I always put my bones in a hole also,

so that they will grow into more animals."

Then he dug a hole

and planted the bones from his meat.

Every day the peacock and the fox
came to see if anything was growing.
Soon there were small green plants
where the peacock had planted
his plum seeds.
Nothing grew where the fox had planted
his bones.

"Bones always take a long time
to come up," said the fox.

The peacock laughed at him.
"Sometimes they stay in the ground
for years without ever coming up."

Weeks passed.
Still the two friends came every day
to look at their garden.
The peacock's plum trees
grew bigger and bigger.
Nothing at all happened
to the fox's bones.
The fox felt more and more foolish.
At last the plum trees
were full of dark red plums.
The peacock feasted on them.
"It's too bad your bones did not grow,"
he said.
"I have so many good plums to eat.
Wouldn't you like some?"
He knew very well
that foxes do not eat plums.

"You know I can't eat plums,"
said the fox,
"but I *can* eat *you!*"
He leaped at the peacock,
but he was too late.
The peacock had flown away.

From then on
the peacock stayed away from foxes.
The fox stayed away from peacocks, too,
except when he could eat one.
And he never again planted bones.

The
Stupid Fox

Once a tiger was caught in a trap.
A man came walking by.
"Brother, help me!" called the tiger.
The man stopped.
"Please let me out of this trap!"
said the tiger.

The man laughed.
"If I let you out of that trap,
you will eat me!
No, I will not help you, Little Brother."

"How can you think that, Brother?"
asked the tiger.
"If you helped me, how could I eat you?
Oh, I would never, never eat you."

At first the man did not believe him,
but the tiger went on like this
for a long time,
and at last the man was convinced.
"All right, Little Brother," he said.
"I will help you."

So the man opened the door of the trap,
and out came the tiger.
The tiger growled.
"I have been in that trap
for a long, long time.
Now I am very hungry.
I am going to eat you up!"
"But that is not fair," said the man.
"I helped you!
Besides, you promised *not* to eat me."
"Yes, it is fair," said the tiger.
"Everyone knows that tigers eat people
when they get the chance.
You should never have believed me."

43

"Before you eat me,
let us ask someone else if it is fair,"
said the man.
"If he says it is,
then you may go ahead."
"Oh, all right," said the tiger.
So the tiger and the man
walked on together.
After a while they met a fox.
"Brother Fox," said the man,
"please help me.
This tiger was caught in a trap.
He begged me to let him out.
He promised not to eat me,
so I did let him out.
Now he tells me he *is* going to eat me!
Is that fair?"

45

"Let me see," said the fox.
"The tiger put you in a trap.
Is that right?"

"No, no," said the man.
"The tiger was in the trap,
and I let him out."

46

"Oh, yes," said the fox.
"Now I understand.
The tiger was in a trap,
and I let him out."
"No, no," said the man.
"That is not right either."

"Grrrr," said the tiger.

"Now, look here, Fox.

I was in the trap.

This man let me out.

Now I am going to eat him,

and maybe I will eat you, too!"

"Oh, dear," said the fox.

"I think I see now.

The man was in the tiger,

and the trap let him out."

"GRRRRRRRR!" said the tiger.

"Oh, my poor head," said the fox.

"I cannot understand this."

"You stupid fox," said the tiger.

"I will have to show you what happened."

49

So they all went back to the trap.

"See, here is the trap!" said the tiger.

"Oh, yes," said the fox.

"And who was in it?"

"I was," said the tiger.

"But how did you get in?" asked the fox.

"Like this, stupid fox," said the tiger.

He walked back into the trap.

"Now do you see how it was?"

"Was the door open like this?"
asked the fox.

"Of course not," said the tiger,
and he slammed the door closed.
"It was shut, like this."

"Oh, yes, now I see how it was,"
said the fox,
and he locked the door.

"Thank you, Brother Fox," said the man.
"If you had not come along,
I would be inside that tiger.
Instead, the tiger
is back inside the trap,
and that is where he will stay!"

j398
W56f

c.1
7.95

WILDER BRANCH LIBRARY
7140 E. SEVEN MILE ROAD   48234

DETROIT PUBLIC LIBRARY

The number of books that may be
drawn at one time by the card holder
is governed by the reasonable needs of
the reader and the material on hand.
Books for junior readers are subject
to special rules.